P9-COP-033

Silly Millies

Ugh! A Bug!

Ned Crowley

Millbrook Press Minneapolis

Cover photograph courtesy of Animals Animals (© Bill Beatty)

Photographs courtesy of Animals Animals: pp. 1 (© Patti Murray), 3 (© Zig Lesczynski), 4 (© Patti Murray), 5 (bottom © Stephen Dalton), 6 (© Bill Beatty), 8 (© James H. Robinson), 9 (© Michael Fogden), 10 (© Stephen Dalton), 11 (© ABPL Image Library), 12–13 (bottom © Michael Fogden), 14 (top © Michael Fogden), 14 (bottom © Michael Fogden/OSF), 15 (© G. I. Bernard/OSF), 17 (© Color-Pic), 18 (© Fabio Colombini Medeiros), 19 (© Michael Fogden/OSF), 20 (© Jack De Coningh), 22 (© Jorg & Petra Wegner), 23 (© Richard Laval), 24 (© Joyce & Paul Berquist), 25 (© John Anderson), 26–27 (© Patti Murray), 29 (© Patti Murray); Photo Researchers, Inc.: pp. 5 (top © M. H. Sharp), 16 (© Wayne Lawler), 21 (© L. & D. Klein); Peter Arnold, Inc.: p. 7 (© S. J. Krasemann); Nature's Faces: p. 12–13 (top © Parvis M. Pour)

Millbrook Press
A division of Lerner Publishing Group
241 First Avenue North
Minneapolis, Minnesota 55401 U.S.A.

Website address: www.lernerbooks.com

Library of Congress Cataloging-in-Publication Data

Crowley, Ned.
Ugh! : a bug! / written by Ned Crowley.
p. cm.—(Silly Millies)
Summary: Illustrations and simple text describe some unusual characteristics of such insects as grasshoppers, beetles, caterpillars, praying mantis, and more.
ISBN-13: 978-0-7613-3450-7 (lib. bdg.)
ISBN-10: 0-7613-3450-5 (lib. bdg.)
[1. Insects—Fiction.] I. Title. II. Series.
PZ7.C88765Ug 2006 [E]-dc22 2003017948

Manufactured in the United States of America
1 2 3 4 5 6 - DP - 11 10 09 08 07 06

Ugh!
A Bug!

Ugh! A bug!
A bug
A bug
went by!

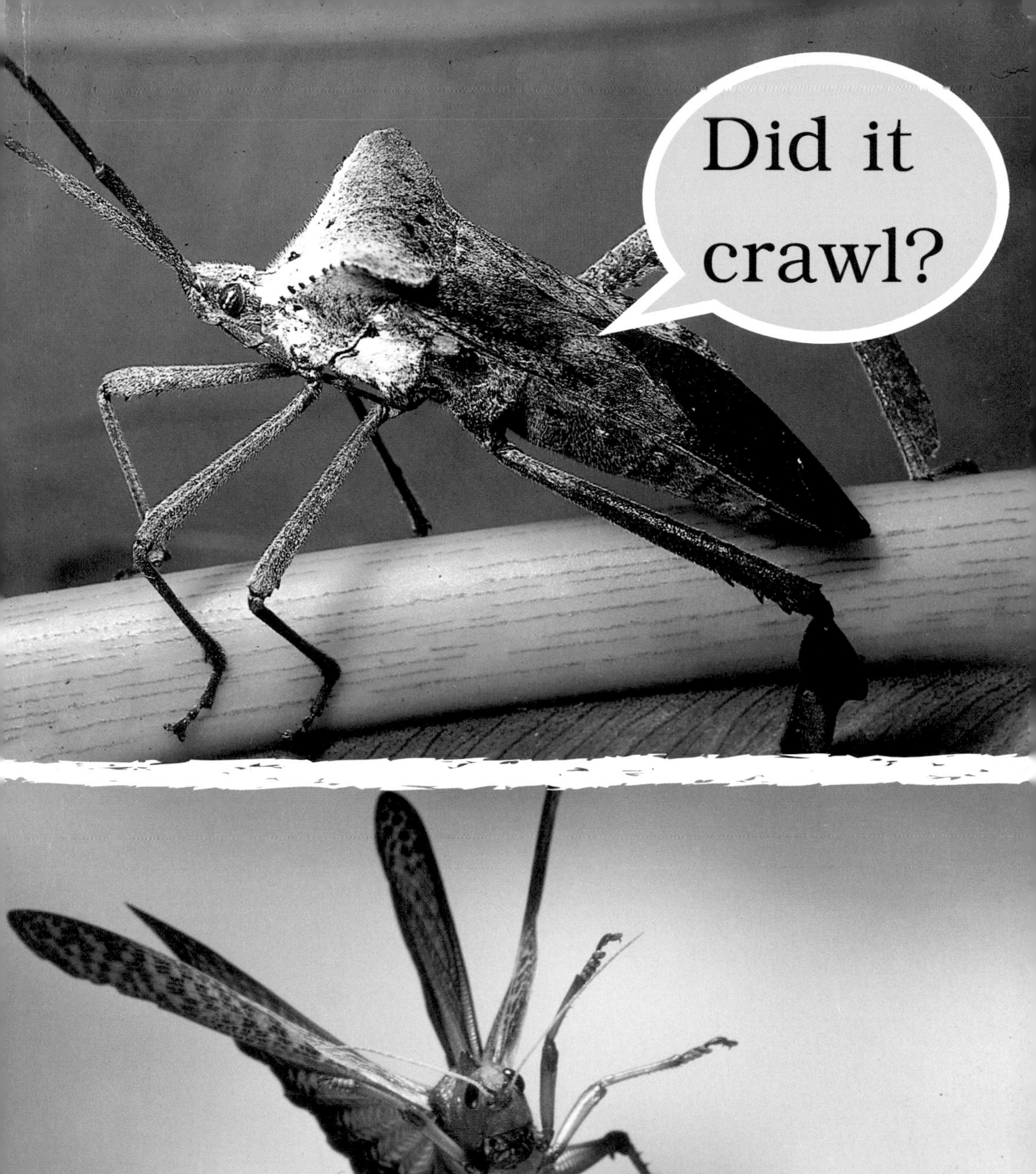

Did it fly?

Was it big?

Was it small?

Was it smooth?

Or not at all?

Did it jump?

Or did
it dig?

Was it
like a
leaf

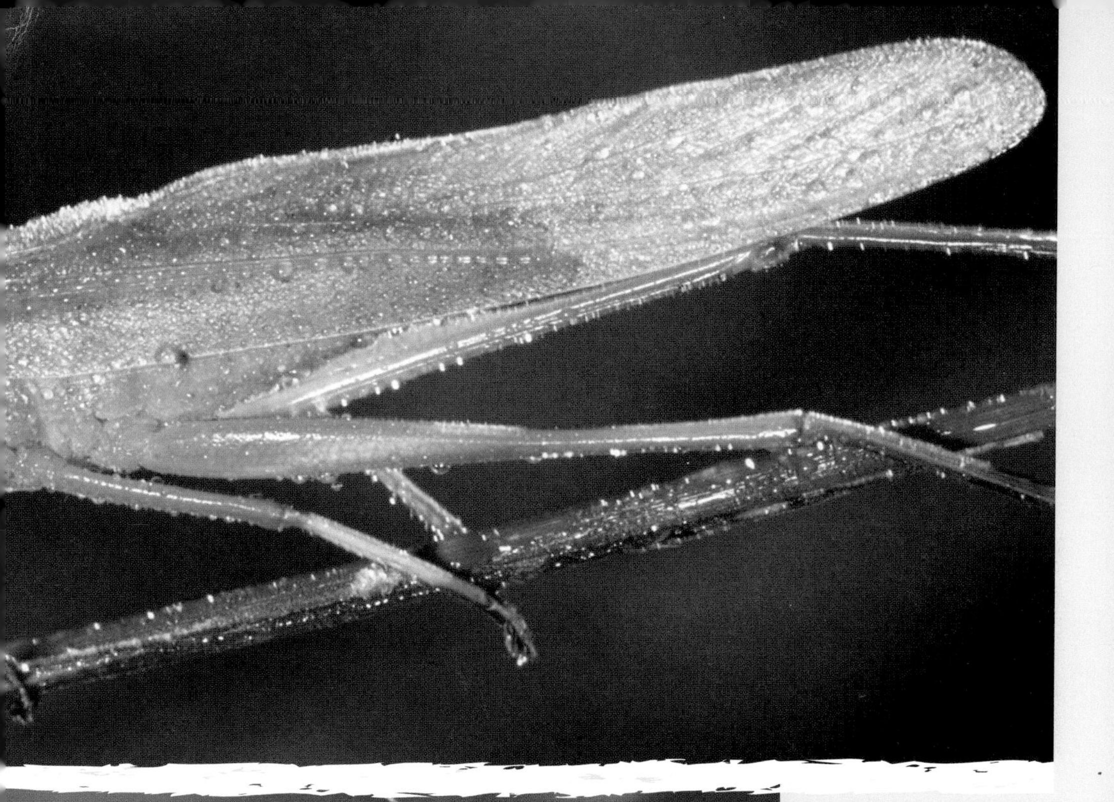

. . . or
twig?

Big eyebrows?
Droopy nose?

Could you count how many toes?

Was it striped?

Or dressed in spots?

Did it
have
teeth?

Did it have lots?

Was it black,

or gold
and
green?

Was it cute,

or was it mean?

Tell us, please, about this bug . . .

this bug that
made you
holler, "Ugh!"

Ugh! It's back and now I see. . .
the bug I saw looks just like me!

What is a Bug?

To be a true bug, you need two things. You need a mouth that pierces and sucks, and you need two sets of wings. One set is hard. The other set is soft. A ladybug is a bug. Some of the creatures in this book are not really bugs. They are insects. Insects don't always have the two things needed to be a bug. So—all bugs are insects, but not all insects are bugs.

Did you Know?

There are more insects on Earth than any other animal.

Insects have a chain of small hearts to pump blood around their bodies.

Flies can taste with their feet.

A dragonfly can fly as fast as 30 miles per hour.

A Little Secret . . .

Remember the caterpillar at the beginning and end of this book? That is not really its face. It is its bottom! Its real face is on the other end. Scientists think this fake face makes the caterpillars look scary to birds. What do you think?

The Bugs in this Book

Page 1
Giraffe-necked Beetle

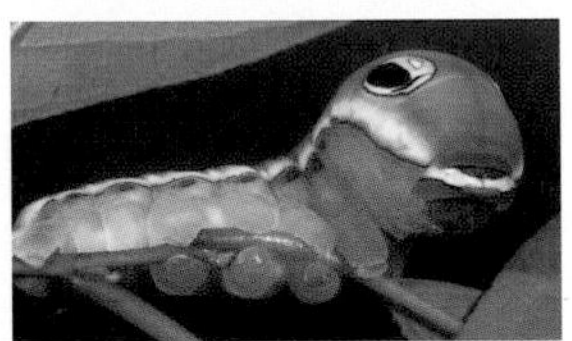

Pages 3, 4, 26, 27, 29
Spicebush Swallowtail
Butterfly Caterpillar

Page 5
Florida Leaf-footed Bug

Page 5
Grasshopper

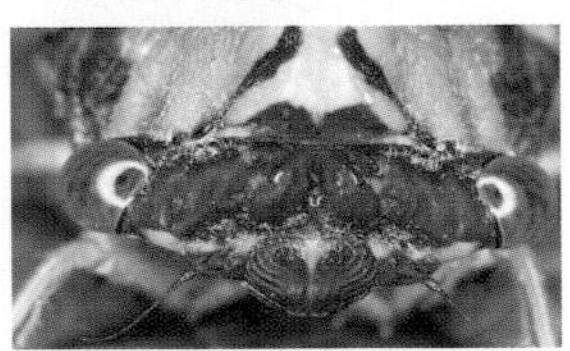

Page 6
Dogday Harvestfly

Page 7
Assassin Bug

Page 8
Pill Bug

Page 9
Spiny Bug

Page 10
Short-horned Grasshopper

Page 11
Tenebnonid Beetle

Page 12
Nebraska Cone-head
Grasshopper

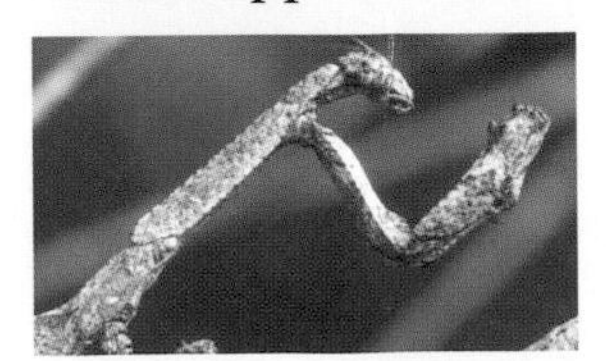

Page 13
Praying Mantis

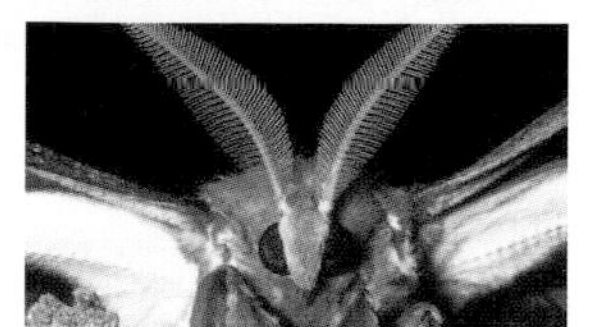
Page 14
Atlas Moth

Page 14
Snouth Beetle

Page 15
Millipede

Page 16
Eupholus Weevil

Page 17
Goliath Beetle

Page 18
Long Horn Beetle

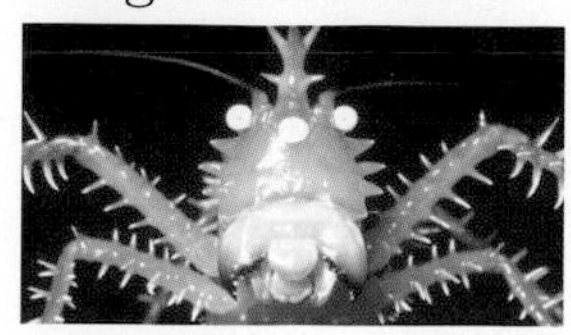
Page 19
Spike-headed Katydid

Page 20
A pair of weevils

Page 21
Colombian Cone-headed Grasshopper

Page 22
Cockchafer Beetle

Page 23
Rainforest Katydid

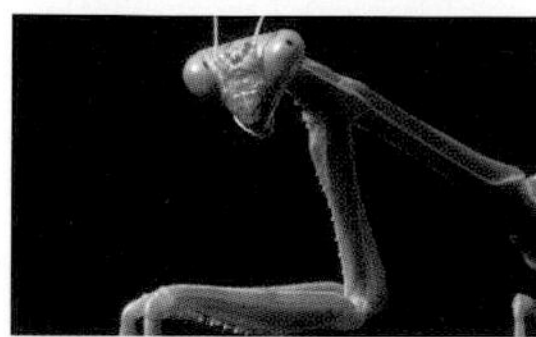
Page 24
Praying Mantis

Page 25
S. E. Lubber Grasshopper

About the Author

Ned Crowley is the author of several children's books including *NaNook & Pryce*, *Aliens Took My Daughter*, and *What's Behind the Bump?*, the last of which he illustrated. Ned's interest in bugs began when someone offered him a nickel to eat one—and he accepted!

In his spare time, Ned works full time in advertising, writing and producing lots of television commercials. He currently lives in Chicago with his wife, Karen, and their three daughters, Shea, Robyn, and Grace.

Tips for Discussion

- Insects look the way they do for a reason. Can you guess why a bug might need long legs, or be green like a leaf, or have a hard shell?

- Have fun designing your own bug. What colors would it be? What kind of eyes? Would it have wings or lots of legs? What silly name could you call your bug?

- Insects can sometimes seem scary, but can you think of ways that insects help us? Name some animals that depend on bugs for food. Why do plants need bugs too?